Graphic design by Jacqueline Paske Gill

ISBN-13: 978-1517605810

ISBN-10: 1517605814

Think Happy Thoughts

by Stephanie Miller

illustrated by Jacqueline Paske Gill

We are fun fairies. We especially like to help children.
Somos hadas divertidas.
Nos gusta especialmente ayundar a los niños.

Not everyone can see or hear us but you can.

No todo el mundo puede vernos ni oírnos, pero usted puede.

Close your eyes and see if you can see us.

Cierra tus ojos y ve si se puedes vernos.

We want you to feel good and be happy.

Queremos que te sientas bien y seas feliz.

To be happy think happy thoughts.

Ser feliz teniedo pensamientos felices.

What are some happy thoughts?

¿Cuáles son algunos pernsmientos felices?

What happy thoughts make you happy now?

Qué pensamientos te hacen feliz ahora?

a hug?
un brazo?

a soft blanket?

una manta suave?

a flower?
una flor?

a tree?

un arbol?

a kitty?
un gatito?

a dog?
un perro?

a friend?
un amigo?

someone you love?

alguien que e amé?

a book?
un libro?

something good to eat?
algo bueno para comer?

dancing?
el baile?

sunshine?

el sol?

a favorite place?
un lugar preferido?

If you are sad or angry you will feel better when
Si estas triste o enojado te sentiras mejor cuando

you think about your own happy thoughts.
tengas tuspropios pensamientos felices

The fun fairies do this.
Las hadas de la diversion hacen esto.

The fun fairies always love you,
Las hadas de la diversion siempre te aman,

no matter what.
no importa que.